# THE LEGEND OF LAWSON'S ELEPHANTS

## An Elephantasy

## By Robert Louis Sheehan
## Illustrated by Tom Linton

DOBER DAN PRESS
QUINCY, MASSACHUSETTS

# THE LEGEND OF LAWSON'S ELEPHANTS
## AN ELEPHANTASY

**By Robert Louis Sheehan**
**Illustrated by Tom Linton**

First Edition, First Printing
Published by
Dober Dan Press
River Bay Club, Suite 432
99 Brackett Street, Quincy, MA 02169
sheehanr@bc.edu
fmwww.bc.edu/rl/sheehanr.html

Profits from the sale of this book will be given to
the Scituate Historical Society, the source of much of
the "Lawsoniana" contained in the story.

Cover and book design by Arrow Graphics, Inc.
info@arrow1.com
Printed in China

ISBN: 0-9668584-2-5
Library of Congress Control Number: 2005907689

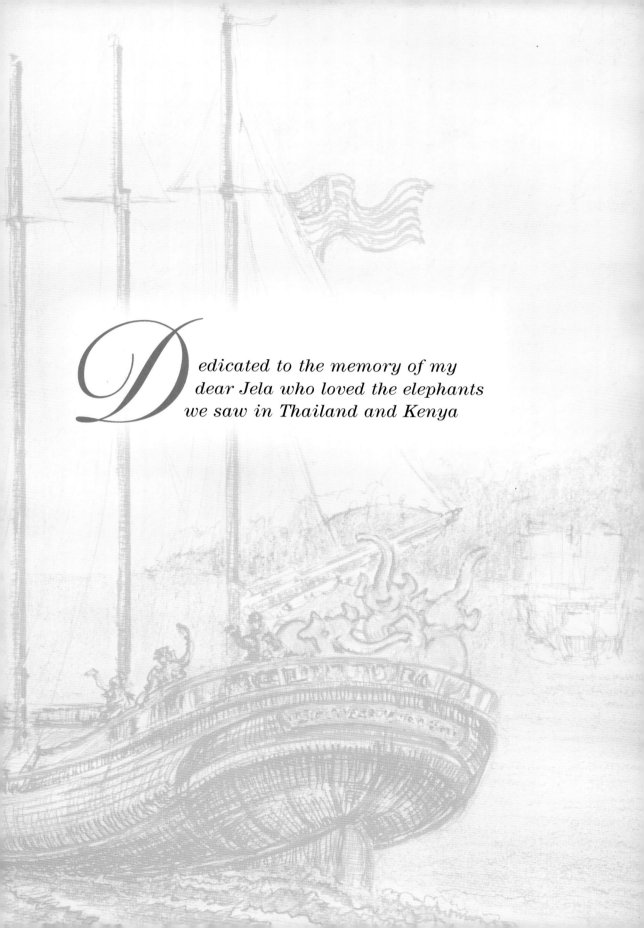

*D*edicated to the memory of my
dear Jela who loved the elephants
we saw in Thailand and Kenya

*M*y name is Nirun and I am one of the three elephants who live on Scituate Common in Massachusetts. My sisters Juntra and Ma Lee live there with me. In English Nirun means "Forever," Juntra means "Moon" and Ma Lee means "Flower." Every day, especially in the summer, all the mothers bring their children to visit us. The children love the fountain that runs over our heads and keeps us cool in the summer. They want to know where the elephants come from and ask many other questions like, "Can the elephants come down from the fountain and play on the grass the way we do?" Yes, we can, but only at night when the whole town lies asleep. Then we come down to eat that sweet grass and play till we get tired.

   I wish I could speak and tell them that myself, because Mamas really don't know how to answer so many of these questions. If I could speak, I would like to tell the children our story, the way their Mamas do when they read other animal stories to them at

bedtime. I would tell them that Juntra, Ma Lee and I came from Thailand, which was once called Siam.

Siam is way across the Pacific Ocean in Asia. In the place where we lived, there was plenty of grass to eat near the river and enough water, so that we could have a drink and spray some on our backs with our trunks whenever we were hot and thirsty. For a while we were very happy living there.

But some of the elephants didn't like us because of our strange golden-brown color. We were different from the others. The bigger elephants didn't bother us very much, but some of the smaller ones used to chase us away from the herd. It became harder every day for us to find fresh grass to eat or a place to drink and spray our backs by the side of the river, and we weren't tall enough to reach up into the trees to find some nice green leaves to eat. So life became more difficult for us.

One day, even some of the bigger elephants joined the smaller ones that were chasing us away from the river. We ran into the woods where they couldn't see us. Finally they left and went back to the river, but now we were lost and couldn't find our way out. We walked one-by-one through the bushes and trees for an hour until we came out onto a road. We didn't know which way to turn to get back to the river.

Just then an old truck came by with two men sitting up front. We had only seen a few people before

along the river and they were Siamese. One of these men was different. He was white, had dark hair, a handsome moustache and a friendly smile. When he saw us he came over to us, and said to the driver, "I have never seen golden-brown elephants before. I would like to take them home with me. I will ask them if they would like to come to America and live on my farm. We have plenty of water and green grass for them." We couldn't understand him, but the Siamese driver told us what he had said. Elephants are very wise, and have good memories. We never forget, especially when people treat us kindly.

We understand human languages very well too, but we cannot speak. All we can do is raise our trunks and make a trumpet sound. But Juntra, Ma Lee and I were too small to make a loud trumpet call. When we raised our trunks to trumpet, our voices were very weak. The other elephants could hardly hear us when we tried to call. "Trumpetooo! Trumpetooo!" we called, especially when we were happy. Because we liked this man from across the sea, we all raised our trunks together and called out "Trumpetooo! Trumpetooo!" as loud as we could. The two men understood that we wanted to go with them and helped us climb onto the back of the truck.

While traveling back to the coast, we learned that the kind man's name was Lawson, known as "Uncle Tom" to children and to his favorite animals. "You will like sailing on my ship, the 'Thomas W. Lawson'," he said. "It is the only ship in the world with seven masts." I looked at Juntra and Juntra looked at Ma

Lee. We didn't know what a mast was, but when we reached the water where his ship was waiting; we could not believe our eyes. We saw this great ship with seven tall tree trunks running one after another from the front to the back. Those were the masts.

At the river we had left behind us, we had only seen a few small boats floating on the water with one or two people on them. Now, when we saw how many people there were on this large ship, we were glad we decided to go with Uncle Tom.

We arrived at the place where the ship was tied up and followed Uncle Tom up onto the deck. All the sailors gathered around to look at us. They had never seen such small elephants like Juntra, Ma Lee and me. Then Uncle Tom took us below the deck to show us where they had plenty of hay and water for all the animals that were going back to the Lawson farm.

The cows and horses didn't mind us. There was enough hay and water for everyone.

Suddenly, as we looked around, the ship shook and began to rock up and down. We heard a lot of noise and voices above and quickly climbed back up to the deck. The captain was giving orders to the sailors. "Hoist the foresail!" he shouted, and then the "mainsail," the "mizzen," the "jigger," the "driver," the "chaser," and finally, the "spanker sail." Slowly, as the captain called out, a beautiful white sail went up on each of the seven masts. The wind quickly filled them out and we began to move swiftly out to sea. Although we were already beginning to understand English, I thought to myself, "more new words, 'above deck, below deck,' and all those names of the seven sails. How confusing!" Uncle Tom knew what I was thinking, and said that he could never get used to those strange names for the seven sails either. "I like to name them for the days of the week: Sunday, Monday, Tuesday, Wednesday, Thursday, Friday, and Saturday." "Days of the week," I thought. "More new words! In Siam, every day was the same to us."

Then Uncle Tom said that we should go below because the wind was strong and the sea was getting rough. We went down below, but we soon got used to

the waves and the ship's rolling from side-to-side and up and down.

I think elephants would make good sailors once we learned how to hoist the sails.

The next day was calm and the sun was shining, so we were allowed to go up on deck again. Uncle Tom told us that he had four daughters and two sons, and he knew that they and all the other children in Scituate would love us. They wouldn't mind that we were different from the other elephants. "Scituate? Where is that?" we wondered. We thought we were going to America. When he saw us looking at one another again, he knew we wanted to know about the farm and this place called Scituate. "Scituate is a beautiful and friendly little town by the sea in Massachusetts which is our state. My farm is very large, nearly a thousand acres, located near the center of the town. I have over 100 very fast horses and a track for them to run on. My cows have plenty of room to find the sweetest grass you could find anywhere in the world." That sounded good to us, so we all raised our trunks and sounded, "Trumpetooo! Trumpetooo!" "My lucky number is 'three'," he continued, "and I know you three elephants will bring me good luck in the future." It pleased us to hear that we would bring good luck to Uncle Tom and that we would have such a beautiful home in the middle of such a friendly little town.

Then Uncle Tom asked us if we would like to take the wheel and steer the ship. "Trumpetooo! Trumpetooo!" we all answered at once. One-by-one we took turns at the wheel. How proud we all were, steering the ship with the wind blowing and the sails above our heads sweeping the "Thomas W. Lawson" through the open sea. Nearly every day, except when the weather was bad, we came up on deck and helped to steer the ship. The sailors all laughed when they saw us at the wheel, but they liked us too, so we were very happy.

One bright morning, Uncle Tom announced that we were heading for Panama and would go through the Canal before going up the coast to Scituate. "Panama? What's that?" we wondered. We thought we were going to Scituate, but now Uncle Tom says

we have to go through the Canal first, and also stop for fresh water. As the sun was setting we reached land and took on more water. We were happy about that because the water on board was running low and we found out that seawater was too salty to drink. Then we sailed up to the Panama Canal, which was a very narrow waterway, not nearly as wide as our river at home. Uncle Tom said, "We are going to cross Panama from the Pacific Ocean to the Caribbean Sea and then to the Atlantic from one big ocean to another big one."

Before we began to move the captain ordered the sailors to lower the sails. We wouldn't need them until we arrived at the other side. As we went through, the water first became higher and the ship rose up with it. Then the water became lower at each stop through the Canal until we reached the Caribbean Sea. "Oh my!" I said to Juntra, "So many new places, and more new words and names to learn!" As usual, Uncle Tom guessed what I was thinking, and said, "Don't worry! It doesn't take long to cross the Caribbean and reach the Atlantic. With these seven sails, we'll be in Scituate in a week."

But we still had a long way to go before reaching Scituate. Uncle Tom said, "First, we'll travel east passing many small islands and then we'll go north until we come to Massachusetts and Scituate Harbor." "East, north? What does that mean?" Juntra said to me. "Until the day we got lost in the woods, the only direction we ever had to know was how to get back to the river." Then one of the sailors said, "I hope it

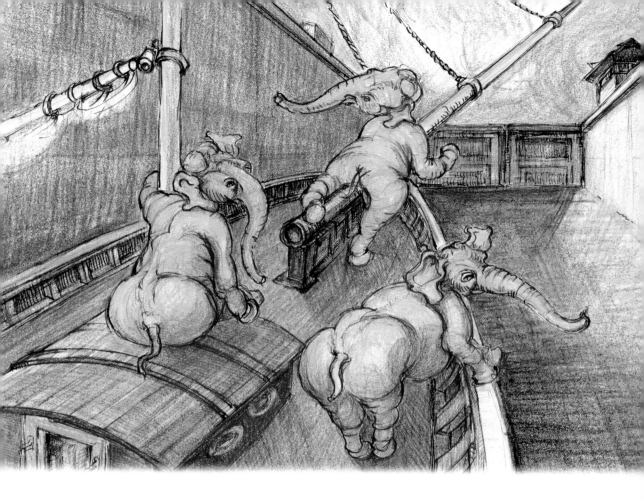

isn't too cold for you in Scituate. The weather gets very cold there, and sometimes it snows, especially in the winter." "Snow? Winter? What are they?" we wondered. We noticed that it did become cooler as we went north, cooler than it ever was in Siam. How could we keep warm when we reached Uncle Tom's farm? In Siam, the weather was always warm, sometimes very hot. So we stayed below where it was warmer than up on the deck.

A few days later, Uncle Tom told us that it was a warm sunny day, and that we should come up on deck as we passed Provincetown and sailed directly across Massachusetts Bay to our new home. An hour

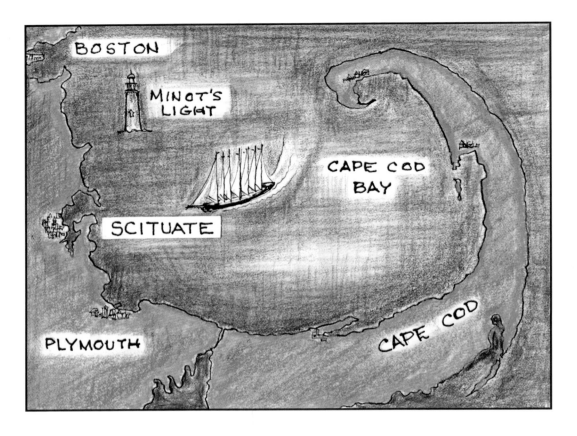

later, Uncle Tom came up beside us and pointed out Scituate Lighthouse as the ship entered beautiful Scituate Harbor. Here many small boats were anchored, but none of them had masts as tall as ours, or sails as big. How proud we were when we saw the huge crowd of people standing on the dock watching as we came in! They all started to clap their hands when they saw us march proudly down the ramp behind our friend Uncle Tom.

"Clear the way!" shouted Uncle Tom, as the crowd gathered around us. "We are going to the farm. Once we rest a little, you can all come out and see our three elephants and the other animals we brought home." Again, we were helped onto the back of a truck and headed over to "Dreamwold," Uncle Tom's farm. As we went up the hill away from the harbor, we wondered what our new home would really be like. Then we went around a bend in the road and suddenly we saw a huge tower. One of the men on the truck with us pointed to the tower and said, "That's Lawson Tower. Uncle Tom had the tower built around the town water tank because he thought the tank was ugly and should be covered. But then he gave the tower to the Town and now people come from everywhere just to see it. Isn't it beautiful?" "Trumpetooo! Trumpetooo!" we all agreed, raising

our trunks as high over our heads as we could. Then we turned our heads toward "Dreamwold," Uncle Tom's home across the way. Out in front of the house was a mast, which was even taller than our seven masts on the ship. On top, a large red, white and blue cloth waved in the breeze. When he saw us looking up at the mast, the man whose name was Lem,

proudly said, "That's the American flag on top of the pole."

The flagpole was cut from the tallest tree, ever taken out of the State of Oregon, 172 feet tall. Again we raised our trunks to greet the flag with our "Trumpetooo! Trumpetooo!" "My goodness," I said again to Juntra and Ma Lee, "there is so much to see and so much to learn!"

Lem brought us into a large barn where we would be staying and where most of the animals lived: horses, cows, dogs and even some sheep and pigs. All of them seemed very friendly except Uncle Tom's English bulldogs. When the bulldogs growled at us, Lem said, "Don't mind them. They are not very pretty, but they will not bite you. Uncle Tom loves them and has won many prizes with them in dog shows all over the country."

In our little stall there was plenty of hay for us and water nearby. But it didn't seem as nice to us as living outside near our river at home, and besides, we were worried that the bulldogs would not want us to live there.

The next day the sun was out and it was warm enough for us to be taken outside to eat the fresh grass. Bulldogs don't eat grass but they began barking at us and growling in an unfriendly way. They were like the elephants who drove us away from the river at home. We decided to go across the field near the fence where they would not notice us, and wait there until Uncle Tom came home from his office in Boston. Suddenly, on top of the fence, we saw a small strange looking animal running along. When he saw us, he stopped, sat up straight and looked at us through eyeglasses, the kind we saw some of the sailors and people on the farm wearing. These glasses were much too big for him, but he didn't seem to mind and kept pushing them up with his paw so that they wouldn't fall off. He looked at us a moment and then said in animal language, "You must be new here. I'm Asquith the Squirrel. Who are you?" Juntra thought he was very impertinent, but she told him our names and said that we had come from Siam on Uncle Tom's seven-masted schooner.

When we told him about our adventure, he replied, "What an interesting story! I shall write it up in English, so that everyone can read it." It was then that we noticed that he held a bird's feather in one of his paws. "This is my pen," Asquith said, holding it up. "It was a seagull's feather that I found on the beach. I have written many stories with it. For ink, I use a black liquid, which was given to me by a friendly octopus who came ashore on North Scituate Beach. The octopus usually uses that inky stuff to hide from his enemies at sea. But he poured some of it into a large clamshell, which I use for an inkwell. That is what I shall use to write down your story in large black letters.

"You know there are some people who think that animals can't learn languages. There is a Harvard professor named Marc Hauser who has studied monkeys, and he says that animals can't learn languages because they don't understand grammar.

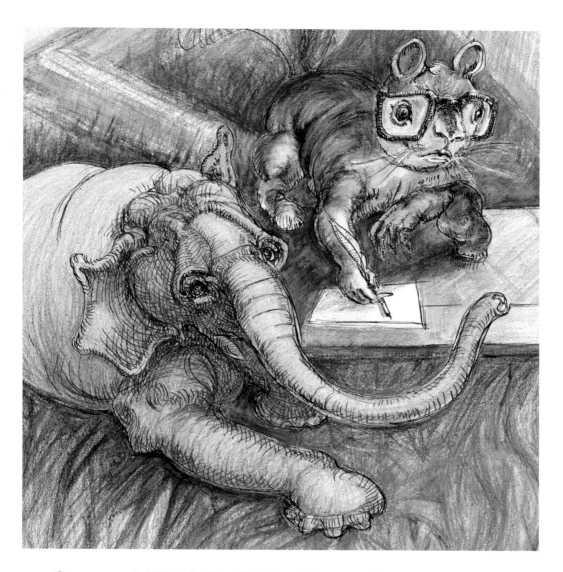

Grammar? What's that? I don't know what grammar is, but I can tell you this, Professor Hauser never studied me, or he would find out that this squirrel learned to write English even if his monkeys could not. My grandfather and my father taught me.

"My grandfather came from Lord Asquith's estate in England. It was quite pleasant living there, but Grandpa wanted to travel. So he hid away on a ship

that was leaving England for America. Grandpa
jumped off the ship at the first stop, which was
Scituate, and lived happily here on Uncle Tom's farm
for the rest of his life," Asquith concluded. Then he
turned around and looked at us through his glasses.
"My grandfather was English, but I am an American
and Americans like short names. So you must call me
'Chuck'." We all thought Chuck was a little strange, a
bit weird, but he seemed so friendly and willing to
help us tell our story that we all answered with a loud
"Trumpetooo!"

How lucky we were, we thought, to have a new
friend like Chuck. When Uncle Tom arrived, Lem told
him that the elephants were unhappy and seemed to

be afraid of the bulldogs. Uncle Tom loved his English bulldogs, but he also wanted us to be happy.

So he said, "Why don't we move you to Scituate Common where you will have plenty of fresh grass to eat? Then we'll build a little pool at your feet where the children can come and play, and a fountain spraying water over your heads so you can keep cool when the weather gets hot. Of course, if you leave the barn, we'll have to build a little house to protect you against the cold winds and the snow in the winter."

"But first," Uncle Tom continued, "my children want to meet you and shake hands with you." The children came across the field to where we were standing, the eldest, Arnold, leading the way. We didn't know anything about "shaking hands," and our feet were too big for the children's little hands, and so as each child came by, we offered our trunks to them.

First Arnold, then Gladys, Marion, Dorothy, Douglas and the youngest Jean, known in the family as "Bunny." How handsome the children were! How glad we were to meet them. We knew that they would always be our friends.

The next day Uncle Tom said he had a surprise for us. We didn't know he had a railroad car of his own with a track leading to the Egypt railroad station nearby. "Every day," he said, "I travel in my own railroad car to and from my office in Boston. Boston is a very large city and I want you to see it. My office is at 333 State Street and my telephone number is 333-3339." Again, we saw how much he loved the number "3" which had brought him such good fortune and now the three of us would bring him luck too. But I wondered what a "telephone" was. Uncle Tom understood me and explained that a telephone is something you can hold up to your ear and talk to someone who is a long way off. I thought how wonderful it would be if we could call the other elephants back at the river in Siam. How sorry they would be that they had chased us away.

Then we went around to the side and sitting on iron tracks we saw a black car with a bell ringing and smoke coming out of the top. "That's the engine that pulls the cars," said Uncle Tom.

"Perhaps one of you could ride up front with the engineer and ring the bell, and the other two could ride in my car with me." Before Juntra and Ma Lee

could answer, I raised my trunk and sounded
"Trumpetooo! Trumpetooo!" The engineer helped me
up on to the train and I took the bell rope in my trunk
and began to ring, Ding Dong! Ding Dong! Juntra and
Ma Lee put their trunks out the window, and sounded,
"Trumpetooo! Trumpetooo!" the three of us ringing
and trumpeting all the way to Boston.

   When we came into South Station, we got off the
train and went out to the street. So many people! So
many tall buildings! People in the streets gathered
around to look at us as we marched from the station
up to 333 State Street, one-by-one, Uncle Tom in the
lead and Lem walking behind us. When we reached

the office, another little bell began to ring. "The telephone. It must be the children calling from home," he said, handing the earpiece to Ma Lee. "They all want to know how you enjoyed your first train ride." "Trumpetooo! Trumpetooo!" we all answered at once. We could hear the children laughing when they heard our call. "Come home soon," said little Bunny.

In the afternoon, before returning to Scituate, Uncle Tom thought we should visit the Boston Common and the Public Garden. In the Garden, we marched along the path where the McCloskey ducks, the Mama duck and her eight little ducklings formed a line. The children were all sitting on the ducks while their parents took pictures of them. When they saw us going by, some of the children jumped off the ducks and tried to climb on our backs. We were afraid to have anyone climb on us because in Siam elephants who have someone sitting on their backs have to work hard all day bringing logs out of the forest. So we ran away from them until we reached the pond where the swan boats were. There they offered us a ride around the pond on one of the swan boats. We wanted to drive the boat, but our legs were too short to reach the pedals.

The pilot said that we could sit near him as he pedaled the boat filled with little children around the pond. What a nice day, we thought, and how lucky the Boston children are to have such a beautiful Garden!

Once he makes up his mind to do something, Uncle Tom always acts very quickly. In a few days,

the pool and the fountain in the middle of Scituate
Common were ready for us to move over there to our
new home. "The weather is still warm," said Uncle
Tom, "but in the winter we'll have a little house built
to protect you from the wind and snow. You have
never seen all of our animals in this part of the world,
especially the bears. Bears have to sleep all winter in
a cave or some other place where it is warm. Like
them, you will learn to sleep in the winter and come
out again in the spring when the weather gets warm."
Juntra, Ma Lee and I looked at each other, and
suddenly we were afraid. "Sleep all winter like the
bears? Not have any nice green grass to eat or water

to drink until the spring? Maybe we should never have left Siam." "Don't be frightened," said Uncle Tom. "You will have a nice long rest in the winter, and then we'll have plenty of grass and water for you when you come out of your little house in the spring." Because we knew Uncle Tom was honest, and always kept his promises, we nodded our heads from side to side and up and down until he saw that we were willing to try to sleep in our little house during the winter, and then come out to play in the sun as soon as the snow is gone in the spring.

And that is what we do every winter: sleep in our little house and then come out in the spring rested, but very hungry and waiting to see our little friends playing in our pool again. We like that very much. There are beautiful pictures of flowers and birds on three of the outside walls of our house, and *my* picture is on the front. My sisters always say that I like to show off by getting out front and raising my trunk way up high whenever the tourists come around to take our picture. Well, maybe, but Ma Lee and Juntra like to have their pictures taken too!

We hope that the carpenters from Public Works will build a slanted roof on the house. That will give us a little more room and help to make the rain and snow slide off in the winter.

The only thing we didn't like was that in June when school is over, some of the boys used to come around and try to steal us from our stand in the park. One time, I hurt my foot when they tried to take me away and a kindly man bandaged the foot, and

brought me to the town Public Works Department until I was well enough to go back to my sisters and to our friendly Scituate children in the park.

Since the last time we were stolen away, all the Scituate school children have promised to protect us and never permit anyone to hurt us again.

After several years in the park, we have many good friends in Scituate and in nearby towns. How sad the children were when we were stolen away, but delighted when we were brought back again! Besides the children, there are friends like Tom Chessia, who, following the tradition of his parents Carl and Jane Chessia, has become a true friend. Tom loves to tell the story of Uncle Tom's elephants to people around Scituate and elsewhere. We have other friends like Pamela Giovannini, the lady in the bookstore, who says she always misses us after we have entered our little house in the winter, and longs for the day in spring when it is warm enough for us to come out again.

George Story, head of the Public Works Department always looks after us, and so do his staff members who took care of us when we were injured and then brought us back to our home in the park. We always remember how kind Bob DeVito, Bill Monahan, Bob Sylvester, Fran Lydon, Larry Jenkins and others were at that time and have been ever since. Another good friend is Barbara Sullivan of the "Beautification Committee." Aided by Judy Mullin and Joan Barbary she painted those beautiful scenes of flowers, birds and blue skies on the outside of our winter home. Those pictures give hope to everyone who sees them, hope that we will have an early spring. We also love the exotic flowers that Barbara plants around our pool in the summer. Those plants remind us of our home by the river in Siam. How happy we are that "Chuck" Asquith has written our story so nicely that people everywhere will understand it and appreciate it.

I hope you children will come to Scituate to visit us when the weather is warm. On very hot days, we will cool you off with a nice spray over your heads from our fountain. Please come and see us!

# Post Script

Nirun, Juntra, and Ma Lee have given me permission to write here on their behalf. They want to thank all of the people who worked so creatively on their book. First of all Boston College professors, Michael J. Connolly and Richard A. Jenson used their well-known computer magic to bring the book text and illustrations to final production. The elephants are grateful to them and to my niece Nancy Sheehan who suggested they introduce the learned squirrel, Asquith, into the story, so that he could transcribe it into English for them. Nor could they forget to thank Alvart Badalian and Aramais Andonian, their book-producer-designers from Arrow Graphics, who combined their professional skills with personal interest in the story, and showed such great patience with Asquith and the rest of us as the story was prepared for publication. My friend Ethel McCool of Scituate also contributed by reviewing the manuscript from its inception, and by taking such excellent photos of the elephants, that artist Tom Linton had the models to create his beautiful illustrations. The elephants want to thank Vera Lee who read the text and thought their story was "darling." Finally, they wish to thank Restaurateur, Chris Chanpreechakul of "Sweet Lemons" Thai restaurant in Weymouth, for suggesting such appropriate Siamese names for the elephants.

The editorial Board, consisting of Nirun and "Chuck" Asquith, recommends this book for the entertainment of children from five to one hundred and five years of age.

*Robert Louis Sheehan*